Pearlie and the Flamenco Fairy

WENDY HARMER

Illustrated by Gypsy Taylor

RANDOM HOUSE AUSTRALIA

For my very own dark-eyed Señorita, Miss Helen xxx.

A Random House book
Published by Random House Australia Pty Ltd
Level 3, 100 Pacific Highway, North Sydney NSW 2060
www.randomhouse.com.au

First published by Random House Australia in 2012
Copyright © Out of Harms Way Pty Ltd 2012

Addresses for companies within the Random House Group can be found
at www.randomhouse.com.au/offices.
National Library of Australia

Cataloguing-in-Publication Entry
    Harmer, Wendy
    Pearlie and the Flamenco Fairy / Wendy Harmer;
    illustrator Gypsy Taylor
    ISBN 978 1 74275 540 3 (pbk.)
    Series: Harmer, Wendy. Pearlie the park fairy; 15
    Target audience: Pre school age
    Subjects: Fairies – Juvenile fiction
              Flamenco – Juvenile fiction
              Madrid (Spain) – Juvenile fiction
    Other authors/contributors: Taylor, Gypsy
    A823.3

Designed and typeset by Jobi Murphy
Printed and bound in China by Everbest Printing Ltd

It was a bright and beautiful afternoon when Pearlie flew into sunny Spain.

From the back of Queen Emerald's magic ladybird she had a wonderful view of the plazas, fountains and the royal palace in the lovely old city of Madrid.

She spotted the patch of green that was the Real Jardín Botánico.

'Hurly-burly! There it is,' she exclaimed. 'That's the Royal Botanic Garden where Florentina lives.'

The ladybird set Pearlie down at the feet of a large statue and flew away.

Suddenly, from behind a bush, out jumped a fairy with long dark hair, sparkling brown eyes and a swirling scarlet skirt.

'*Hola*, Señorita Pearlie!' she cried. She tapped the tips of her shoes on the stone path, twirled, clicked her fingers and shouted, '*Olé!*'

Pearlie clicked her fingers too and shouted back,
'Hooray!'

The two new friends hugged each other.

'I have a wonderful surprise for you!' Florentina said happily. 'I hope you brought your *zapatos de baile*.'

'Pardon?' said Pearlie.

'Your dancing shoes.' Florentina smiled. 'Tonight I am giving a special party in your honour. A dance party! And everyone will be there to meet you.'

Now, Pearlie had her boots and her slippers with her, but she had not brought any dancing shoes.

Pearlie could sing and fly like a bird. Everyone said so. But as for dancing?

Pearlie's cheeks turned bright pink. 'Um, I'm not very good at ...' she started to say.

Florentina beamed at Pearlie, spun on her heels and said, *'No hay problema!'*

Florentina picked up Pearlie's bag and tap-tapped away along the path. Pearlie followed, wondering what would happen when all of Spain saw that she had two left feet.

Soon the fairies came to a wonderful shady pergola.

Fairy Florentina rummaged in her bag and handed Pearlie a pair of shiny black shoes.

'Here, put these on,' she said. 'Hurry. Señor Philippe will be here *en un momento.*'

As Pearlie buckled on Florentina's shoes, she heard a clicketty-clack, clicketty-clack echoing across the marble floor.

Striding towards her was a tall and handsome fellow. His eyes were big and black, his two long antennae were twitching and he wore a splendid moustache. Two of his six thin legs ended in shiny shoes.

He was a very sleek Spanish cricket!

'It's Señor Philippe,' whispered Florentina. 'He is here to teach us the flamenco!'

'Flamenco? What's that?' asked Pearlie.

'It is the dance of FIRE!' Señor Philippe shouted as he stopped in front of her. 'We stamp our feet and dance for the joy of life! I am here to teach you THE DANCE!'

Pearlie thought that all sounded very nice, but she was a bit tired after her long trip from Jubilee Park.

'Perhaps I could have a cup of tea?' she asked.

'NEVER!' Philippe boomed. 'We are never too tired to dance the flamenco.'

The next moment there was music and a voice wailing 'Aiyeeee! Aiyeeee!' Pearlie saw a small beetle bent over a guitar and singing his heart out.

'Raise your arms like this!' said Florentina. 'Follow me!'

And away she went, madly tapping her toes and fluttering her skirts, just like the frilly petals on a red carnation.

'Twirly-whirly!' gasped Pearlie.

Señor Philippe clapped loudly. 'It is your turn, *señorita*. Go!'

Pearlie stepped out and tried her best to keep in time with the music but soon she had her feet and wings all tangled up.

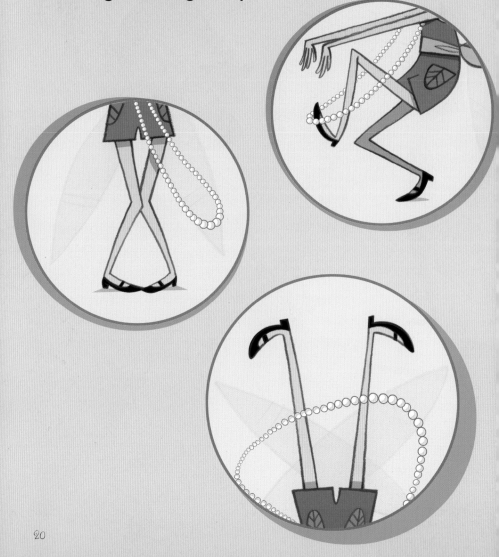

'No, no, no!' said Señor Philippe. '*Otra vez!* Again!'

All afternoon Pearlie tried her best, but it was no good.

The more Señor Philippe shouted and the faster the guitar played, the more she stumbled and bumbled and thought she might fall over.

It was almost dusk and a big round Spanish
moon was rising when the lesson was over
at last. By now Pearlie was very, very tired.

'You were *magnífico*, my friend,' said Florentina.
'Now, there is time for a rest and when the stars
come out we will go to the dance. Everyone will
be there to meet you.'

Now Pearlie was even more worried. She had
not mastered the flamenco at all, and her poor
feet were tired and throbbing.

Pearlie was glad to sit down as Florentina served a supper of spicy fried potatoes, pickled peppers and slices of olive stuffed with almond.

'We call it tapas. That means lots of little dishes, so you don't get too full to tap your feet,' said Florentina as she poured Pearlie a tall glass of fresh orange juice with cinnamon and honey.

As Pearlie ate every delicious morsel, she almost forgot about her sore feet. Almost. Poor Pearlie would have liked to go to bed and sleep the night away.

But Florentina had been so kind and was so excited. Pearlie must dance the dance of FIRE. *Olé!*

Soon it was time to go. Florentina changed into another beautiful swirling gown covered with lace and frills. It was even more spectacular than the last. Pearlie didn't have anything like it in her bag.

'You can borrow one of mine,' said Florentina.

The dress was black and red and very grand, but somehow didn't quite suit Pearlie who, it must be said, always looked her best in pink.

'Do you mind?' asked Pearlie as she raised her wand.

'*Nada!* Not at all!' laughed Florentina. 'Your dress must be just as you wish.'

With a wave of Pearlie's magic wand, the gown was instantly layers and layers of lovely pink.

'One more thing,' said Florentina, producing her own wand.

It had a red ruby on top, and with one flourish, Pearlie's dress was covered in polka dots. Even her shoes were spotty! On her head she wore a beautiful lace veil and a pink carnation.

'*Maravilloso!*' cried Florentina. 'Let's go dancing!'

'Taps and twirls!' Pearlie wailed. 'I'm really not very good at …'

But the flighty Florentina had already hurried off and, once again, Pearlie chased after her.

The moon was bright and the stars were twinkling on the fairy flamenco dance. It was an extraordinary sight! All the fairies of Spain were there.

The music was loud and fast. On the white marble dance floor skirts flew as feet tapped ever-faster. The sight of it made Pearlie feel dizzy.

All around them was a clicking noise that sounded like the call of cicadas in summer back home in Jubilee Park.

'They're castanets,' explained Florentina. 'We use them to keep the beat, from our fingers to our feet.'

Then she jumped up and joined the crowd, snapping her castanets all the way.

Pearlie was watching everything and very much hoping that no-one would ask her to dance, when she saw Señor Philippe coming towards her with his hand outstretched.

'Time for you to show everything you have learned about the flamenco,' he said, smiling through his big moustache. *'Vamos a bailar! Let's dance.'*

Pearlie's heart sank to the floor. But to refuse the invitation from Señor Philippe would be very bad manners indeed. And she did so want to make fairy Florentina happy.

She stood up and …

… Oh dear!

Pearlie's feet tangled in her long, flowing skirt.

She tripped and fell on her wand.

The top of it broke off with a loud 'snap' and every one of its precious pearls scattered and bounced across the floor.

Boink, boink, boink. Clatter!

'Hurly-burly!' cried Pearlie. What if the pearls got under the feet of the dancers? What if they skidded and fell over?

That would be awful.

In a flash, Pearlie went after her shiny pearls. She darted this way and that between the feet of the fairy dancers.

She flew up and down and round about. One by one, she scooped the pearls from the floor and held them in her tiny hand.

'Click, clack,' they rattled, like pearly castanets.

She darted this way and that, finding one pearl and then another.

One, two, three, four, five, six ... She almost had them all.

Then Pearlie saw from the corner of her eye that the Spanish fairies were hurrying from the dance floor.

They stood and watched in amazement as Pearlie whirled and twirled in the air. Her wings flashed in the moonlight and her spotty skirts tossed and tumbled.

Seven, eight, nine … Stars and moonbeams!

At last she had them all.

Then all the Spanish fairies began to stamp their feet, clap their hands and shout: *'Olé! Olé! Olé!'*

Señor Philippe was astounded.

'*Estupendo! Magnífico!*' he said. 'Never have I seen the flamenco danced quite like this, Señorita Pearlie.'

'*Bien hecho.* Well done!' laughed fairy Florentina. 'You certainly showed everyone here a thing or two.'

Pearlie was very pleased. She blushed the same colour as the flower in her hair.

But there was still the problem of her broken wand and her handful of pearls.

'*Lo siento*. I'm so sorry,' Florentina said sweetly. 'But we will have your wand fixed as soon as we can. *Rápidamente!* Until then, please use my red ruby wand for your stay here in Spain. It has special powers, as you will see.'

And do you know? That red ruby wand was very special.

Everywhere Pearlie went in the gardens of Spain, she only had to wave it and all the flowers would ruffle their petals, sing and dance for her.

It was the most magical summer ever.

When the petals on the flowers began to fall, it was time for Pearlie to leave. Señorita Florentina presented Pearlie with her own wand, fixed and good as new.

'Always remember, Pearlie,' she said. 'Everyone can dance. One must always dance like no-one is watching. The flamenco comes straight from the heart and you have a very big heart.'

Pearlie vowed to always remember what Florentina had said.

And as she flew up and away from the gardens of Spain, her heart was tapping a wild and wonderful flamenco beat.